S.W.I.T.C.H.

SERUM WHICH INSTIGATES TOTAL CELLULAR HIJACK

Other books in the S.W.I.T.C.H. series:

S.W.I.T.C.H.

SERUM WHICH INSTIGATES TOTAL CELLULAR HIJACK

Beetle Blast

Ali Sparkes

illustrated by
Ross Collins

OXFORD
UNIVERSITY PRESS

OXFORD
UNIVERSITY PRESS

Great Clarendon Street, Oxford OX2 6DP

Oxford University Press is a department of the University of Oxford.
It furthers the University's objective of excellence in research, scholarship,
and education by publishing worldwide in

Oxford   New York

Auckland   Cape Town   Dar es Salaam   Hong Kong   Karachi
Kuala Lumpur   Madrid   Melbourne   Mexico City   Nairobi
New Delhi   Shanghai   Taipei   Toronto

With offices in

Argentina   Austria   Brazil   Chile   Czech Republic   France   Greece
Guatemala   Hungary   Italy   Japan   Poland   Portugal   Singapore
South Korea   Switzerland   Thailand   Turkey   Ukraine   Vietnam

Oxford is a registered trade mark of Oxford University Press
in the UK and in certain other countries

Text © Ali Sparkes 2011
Illustrations © Ross Collins
S.W.I.T.C.H. logo designed by Dynamo Ltd

British Library Cataloguing in Publication Data
Data available

ISBN: 978-0-19-2729378
1 3 5 7 9 10 8 6 4 2

For Freddie (junior)

Danny and Josh
(and Piddle)

They might be twins but they're NOT the same! Josh loves insects, spiders, beetles and bugs. Danny can't stand them. Anything little with multiple legs freaks him out. So sharing a bedroom with Josh can be . . . erm . . . interesting. Mind you, they both love putting earwigs in big sister Jenny's pants drawer . . .

Danny

- FULL NAME: Danny Phillips
- AGE: 8 years
- HEIGHT: Taller than Josh
- FAVOURITE THING: Skateboarding
- WORST THING: Creepy-crawlies and tidying
- AMBITION: To be a stunt man

Josh

- FULL NAME: Josh Phillips
- AGE: 8 years
- HEIGHT: Taller than Danny
- FAVOURITE THING: Collecting insects
- WORST THING: Skateboarding
- AMBITION: To be an entomologist

Piddle

- FULL NAME: Piddle the dog Phillips
- AGE: 2 dog years
  (14 in human years)
- HEIGHT: Not very
- FAVOURITE THING: Chasing sticks
- WORST THING: Cats
- AMBITION: To bite a squirrel

CONTENTS

Let Them Eat Cake

By the time the toxic cloud reached him it was already too late. Josh went cross-eyed, grabbed his throat and gurgled. He slumped onto the bed, his face going purple.

'Mmm—mmm—muuu,' he rasped.

His poisoner stood over him, smirking; immune to the gas.

'Muuu—' gasped Josh, falling off the bed and crawling towards the door. 'MUM! Danny's guffing at me again!'

Danny grinned proudly as his twin brother fell out onto the landing, sucking in grateful breaths of clean air.

Mum was less amused. She put her head round their bedroom door and then withdrew it again, smartish.

'Danny! That's revolting! Go to the toilet at once!' she called from the other side of the door. 'Good grief! What is going on in your innards?'

'It's you that feeds me,' pointed out Danny.

'Don't be cheeky!' snapped Mum.

'It's OK—I've stopped now,' said Danny, stepping out to see his twin slumped against the banisters, flapping a hand in front of his face.

'Well I hope so!' said Mum. 'I don't want you embarrassing Josh at the Wild Things meeting.'

Danny blinked in surprise. 'Wild Things? I don't go to Wild Things! *I'm* not the freaky little bug boffin. That's just Josh!'

Josh might be identical to Danny on the outside (although a lot less fluffy on the hair front and without the skater-boy clothes) but on the inside the brothers couldn't have been more different, thought Danny. He loved loud music and skateboarding and kicking footballs around, while Josh loved peering at nature through a magnifying glass. That's why he'd signed up for Wild Things and had started to go every week, with a load of other freaky little bug boffins. Danny had no intention of joining him!

'I'm sorry, but you *have* to go,' said Mum, taking some towels into the bathroom. 'Your football coach rang to say practice is cancelled and I'm going to pick up my new car, so there's nobody to look after you. You're going with Josh.'

'Oh *no*!' wailed Josh. 'He's going to guff all the way through!'

'Ah well,' sighed Danny. 'I'll just have to set up my own Wild Things gang—the Stink Bugs.'

'Just *try* to act interested,' hissed Josh as he and Danny joined the other Wild Things at the

13

Blackthorn Wildlife Centre. They met every
Monday after school to do experiments and nature
trails and look at things through microscopes.
Today they were going pond dipping to see what
they could find.

'Danny, meet Ollie, Milo, Biff, and Poppy,' said
Josh, pointing to each of his fellow bug boffins
in turn. They all wore 'nature freak' clothes,
Danny noticed. Lots of green and brown and little
sleeveless jackets with loads of pockets—just
like Josh. Danny, in his bright orange sweatshirt
and baseball cap, looked like a traffic cone by a
hedgerow.

'Hi, Danny,' said Biff, who had a pair of binoculars round his neck.

'Greetings,' said Ollie and Milo, together. They both had spectacles and funny green hats, like pensioners wore in the garden.

'Hi, Danny, nithe to meet you,' lisped Poppy, who had brown plaits, freckles, and a rather alarming number of teeth. She rattled a little plastic tub at him and whispered, 'Antth' eggths!' with her eyebrows going up and down.

'Er . . . yeah,' said Danny, backing away.

'Look—Grandadth come to help today,' said Poppy, pointing to a tall man in a low-brimmed hat who was standing nearby, gazing out of the window. Danny noticed he had a strange, black, pointed fingernail on the little finger of his left hand. Well, weirdness obviously ran in the family.

'I think she likes you,' sniggered Josh, as Poppy smiled scarily at Danny and stroked the lid of her plastic tub. 'She wants to take you home . . . '

'Shut up!' hissed Danny, and hurried away towards some interesting buttons near a collection of wildlife pictures. They made wildlife-y noises

when he pressed them. *Ribbit.* 'Toad,' said Danny.
Chirrup. 'Grasshopper,' said Danny. *Zzzzzzz.*
'Bluebottle.'

'See,' said Josh. 'You're quite good at this stuff.'

'Only because . . . ' said Danny, ' . . . *we've*
either been one of them or nearly been *eaten* by
one of them.'

'Shhhh!' hissed Josh, looking around uneasily.
'Don't tell everyone!'

'What? That our mad next-door-neighbour
keeps turning us into creepy-crawlies?' said Danny,
making no effort at all to be quiet. 'Yeah, right.
Everyone's going to believe *that*!'

Someone poked Danny hard in the ribs and
went 'Shhhhh, you numbskull! You never know
who might be listening! And I am *not* mad. I am a
genius!'

Danny and Josh spun round, gaping with shock.
There stood Petty Potts, the old lady from next
door. In her tweedy hat and glasses, carrying a
straw bag and smiling sweetly, you would never
guess what she truly was—a brilliant scientist
with a secret laboratory hidden beneath her

garden shed. Earlier that year Josh and Danny had stumbled into it while she was in the middle of one of her astonishing experiments—to change things into creepy-crawlies.

They had got caught up in a jet of her SWITCH spray and shortly afterwards morphed into spiders. Which was a bit of a shock. It was a small miracle that they hadn't been squashed flat, drowned, or eaten. And since then, despite trying really hard to steer clear of any further spraying, they had each been turned into a bluebottle, a grasshopper, an ant, and a daddy-long-legs. Thankfully, only temporarily.

'What are *you* doing here?' spluttered Josh.

'It's a free country!' said Petty. 'I'm allowed into my local wildlife centre, aren't I?'

Danny eyed her bag nervously, looking for the telltale plastic spray bottle.

'You needn't look so petrified, Danny!' she said. 'I haven't got any SWITCH spray with me today.'

Danny sighed with relief. It wasn't so much the 'being a creepy-crawly' he minded—more the 'nearly being eaten' so very often. He'd also once spent more time than he wanted to remember hiding in a cat's ear while he was a grasshopper. And he was haunted still by the things he'd eaten when he was a bluebottle.

'No,' said Petty, reaching into her bag and pulling out a small tin. 'No spray today. This time it's in pellet form. I want to SWITCH a rat. I need to try out more mammals—other than you two. I'm going to hide the pellets in some food!' She leaned in towards them and whispered, 'Don't forget to keep looking out for the REPTOSWITCH cube! Only one more to find.' She looked edgily around her. 'And never forget you might be being

watched! Victor Crouch's people are everywhere!'
And she strode off, before Danny or Josh could say
anything else.

Josh shrugged. 'Well, at least there's no chance
we'll get caught out by *pellets*,' he said. 'Let's just
pretend we don't know her.'

'She's never going to let up about that blinkin'
cube, is she?' muttered Danny. 'We've found four
of them and she already had one—you'd think
she'd be happy with that!'

'Yes—but without the *last* cube, she can't work
out the REPTOSWITCH code, can she?' said Josh.
'And without the code she'll never be able to
make the spray and we'll never get a chance to be
alligators or snakes.'

Josh and Danny looked at each other and
bit their identical lips. Although most of their
adventures as creepy-crawlies had been terrifying,
they'd also been exciting and, at times, quite
brilliant. Both boys knew how it felt to fly, to leap
twenty times their own body-length, to run up
walls, and walk upside down along ceilings. It was
just the nearly getting killed . . .

But being a reptile would be different! Most reptiles were tough and much, much bigger than a creepy-crawly. It would be amazing to become a big scaly predator! That was why they had agreed to help Petty find her missing cubes, so she could crack the REPTOSWITCH code.

'Come on,' said Josh. 'We're not going to worry about the last cube here. She's hardly going to have hidden it half a mile from her house.'

'We're not going to worry about being watched by government spies, either,' grinned Danny. 'All that *"Victor Crouch is after me"* business! *That's* all in her head!'

The Wild Things went to scoop creatures out of the pond. Danny mooched along after them, bored and trying not to notice Poppy smiling and waving at him with her little glass jar on a bit of pink string. He did *not* want to get to know a dragonfly nymph or a newt—or Poppy. It was a stupid waste of time. He sat down at a picnic bench while the others squelched about by the edge of the water, ooohing and aaahing about tiny splodgy brown life-forms.

Danny's stomach rumbled. He noticed a plate left on the table. On it was a sticky chocolate muffin bought from the wildlife centre café. With just a bit broken off. A rich sweet chocolatey smell was wafting across from it. Danny's mouth watered. He looked around to see if anyone was coming to claim it. Nobody seemed to be. He peered at it a little closer. No wasps on it.

Another chocolatey waft reached him. Danny couldn't resist. He grabbed the abandoned cake and bit into it. 'Mmmmm-mmmm,' he groaned, happily.

'Danny! Come and see this!' said Josh,
crouching in some bog weed. The other Wild
Things had wandered off to the other end of the
c-shaped pond, and were on the far side of some
bushes. Danny felt he could bear to show some
interest with Poppy no longer goggling at him.

He took the muffin with him and ambled over.
'See!' said Josh, pointing at a muddy pebble.
'A great crested newt!'
'Hey. Wow.' Danny shrugged.

'What are you eating?' asked Josh, sniffing at his brother.

'Muffin. 'ave some,' said Danny, handing the last chunk to his brother.

Josh held up his muddy hands. 'Stick it in for me, will you?' he said, opening his mouth. Danny shoved it in.

'Mmm, nice chunky chocolate drops,' mumbled Josh.

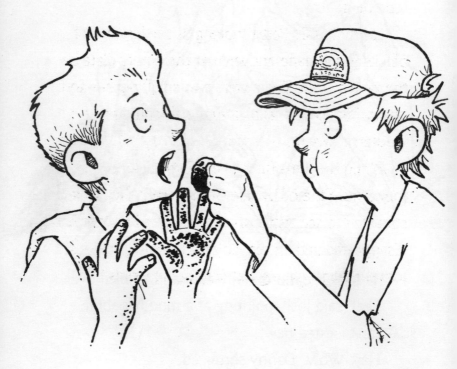

'Hey!' said a sharp voice behind them. 'Who's had my cake?'

Danny spun round, guiltily. Standing by the picnic bench was . . . oh *no* . . . Petty Potts.

Petty stared at him and then at Josh, who had turned round too. 'Oh dear, oh dear, oh dear,' she said, spotting the chocolate crumbs around their mouths.

'What *kind* of oh dear?' asked Josh, sounding a little bit squeaky.

'Ummm,' said Petty, looking at the little tin of pellets in her hand and then at the empty plate on the picnic table. There were two small pops—and no further point in explaining. Josh and Danny wouldn't have understood.

When the remaining Wild Things came round from the other side of the pond, they were surprised to see that Josh and his bored brother had disappeared and an old lady was peering anxiously into the pond, saying not very polite words.

Bottom Breathers

'Don't tell me,' snapped Josh. 'Just don't tell me!' He had his eyes screwed shut and refused to open them.

Danny waggled his feelers in annoyance. 'All right. I won't tell you! You can blummin' well guess!' He climbed up a thick green plant stem and stared down into the mirror reflection of the water below.

'That was the food that Petty put the SWITCH pellets into, *wasn't it*?' huffed Josh, still with his eyes shut. 'She poked them into a chocolate muffin and then you went and ate it! And fed it to me too!'

'Sorry,' said Danny. 'But you should have a look now, you know. This is pretty cool.' His six legs clung to the green blade and he leaned over for a better look. A rather handsome face peered back up at him from his reflection. His eyes were wide apart and grey, like metal buttons, set into a smooth black face which had a shiny grey mouth area with some delicate feelers around it. His body was smooth and gently striped with black and dark brown lines and his legs and under-parts were a rather nice yellow.

'Get these legs!' Danny raised up his chunky back pair which were curved into thick furry segments and felt very powerful. He tried to get a better view of them in the water by leaning off the huge blade of grass a bit further. And then . . .

'Whoooooaaaaah!'

SPLASH!

He was deep under the water.

And Danny couldn't swim.

The SPLASH! made Josh at last open his eyes. He stared in alarm down at the pond below him. He too had arrived in his new creepy-crawly form standing on a wide green leaf, just above the water. The world around him looked totally unlike the normal world. It was absolutely huge, for one

thing. An alien spaceship suddenly swooped past him, making a deafening thrumming noise. Except it *wasn't* a spaceship. It was a dragonfly, with a stunning blue-green body, sparkling wings and a nasty killer instinct.

'Danny!' shouted out Josh, ducking under the leaf for safety, but there was no reply—except a widening ring across the water where something had just fallen in. Something, Josh realized, which was almost certainly Danny.

'Oh no!' wailed Josh, wondering what to do.

Then he caught sight of his reflection, wobbling below him, and found himself laughing. Actually laughing. For once—just for *once*—he and Danny didn't need to be scared! 'It's OK, Danny! I'm coming!' chortled Josh, and dived into the water.

Danny held his breath for as long as he could as he tumbled slowly over and over, sinking down in the green soupy liquid. Fronds of weed brushed against him and wriggling see-through creatures scurried away into the gloom. The water was cool and somehow *thicker* than he remembered. It seemed to slide around him in an odd way and he could see in it perfectly well, now that he was getting used to it. A forest of underwater trees and shrubs waved gently to and fro and a gigantic brown water snail ambled past him up a stem, blowing a large bubble in his face.

I've got to get to the surface! said a panicky voice in his head and he wished he'd tried harder to learn to swim. He was quite a sporty boy, but more of a football and cricket kind.

Suddenly there was a booming noise and all the watery trees and bushes waved extra fast as a body tumbled down from the surface, spun around like a cricket ball, and then began to row quickly towards Danny. Danny stared at it, scared. Meeting other creatures when you were SWITCHed was nearly always highly dangerous.

'Danny? Danny!' shouted the other creature and Danny heaved a huge sigh of relief as he recognized Josh shooting towards him, his voice rather strange and musical through the water.

'Hang on!' said Danny, out loud. 'How can I breathe a huge sigh of relief? I'm under water!'

'Yes—but you're a great diving beetle!' laughed Josh.

'Oh, thanks,' said Danny.

'No—I mean—that's what we're called,' explained Josh. 'We're Great Diving Beetles. We can breathe under water. We carry our own air pocket with us—see.' He jabbed his front leg against his face and Danny saw a silvery line dimple in under it. Yes—it was as if they were travelling in little sacks of oxygen. 'We have to go up to the surface every so often and get more air,' explained Josh. 'We sort of suck it up with . . . well . . . with our bums.'

'OK. Whatever you say, you weirdo—but it's the last time you have a go at me for guffing!' said Danny. He turned in the water, using his strong back legs like his brother was doing. They moved like oars on a rowing boat and scudded him along through the water at great speed. Josh sped along beside him.

'OK—so what's going to eat us?' said Danny, nervously. Something *always* tried to eat them.

'That's the brilliant bit! Nothing!' Josh was grinning with his funny insecty mouth and laughing so much there were tiny air bubbles streaming up from it. 'For once, *we* are the predators!'

'You mean to tell me that there's no big ugly fish coming after us?' said Danny.

'Nope. Because this is a nature pond. There aren't any big goldfish in it. Just little minnows and sticklebacks and frogs and stuff—and *they* won't bother us. And even if they try . . . ' He grinned again, which looked rather alarming on a beetle. ' . . . we've got a secret weapon!'

'What's that then?' asked Danny. 'A sting? Nasty bite?' He'd noticed that Josh's jaws looked pretty fierce.

'You'll see,' said Josh. He spun round and rowed along again. Danny moved with him and then he noticed something long and browny-green scurrying along under a rock.

Danny screamed.

Because Josh was wrong.

Josh had got it *badly* wrong.

Lurking under the rock, staring balefully right at Danny—was a CROCODILE.

Evil Wet Ones

The crocodile loomed towards him, its tail rippling in the water behind it and its pale yellow belly shining through the green gloom.

Danny was terrified. 'CROCODILE!' he screamed and then let off an absolutely rip-snorting guff which bubbled through the water like a mini volcano. 'Eeeeuw!' Danny had never been affected by his own guffs before, but *this* one was truly revolting, and was spreading in an icky warm cloud all around him.

Josh doubled back to see what the rather musical bubbling noise was. 'Ah,' he said. 'You've found your secret weapon, then.'

'CROCODILE!' gurgled Danny. But the crocodile was swimming away. Fast.

'Yup,' said Josh. 'When you think you're being

attacked by a predator you can let off a really evil
wet one. Another reason the fish don't fancy you
much.'

'*I* don't fancy me much!' gasped Danny, getting
his back legs going and powering away from
his cloud of stinky wet guff. 'But Josh—what
about the crocodile? You said we didn't have any
predators!'

'You donkey!' laughed Josh. 'That was a newt!'

'But . . .'

'You could eat *him* if you really wanted to.'

'But . . . why do we need the killer guffs if we've
got no predators?'

'Well, we haven't got any predators in *here*,'

said Josh, landing on a large rock and hanging on to it with his rather sticky front feet. 'But we have up *there*.' He looked up through the gloopy skin of the pond's surface which broke into waves and widening rings every so often, and made booming, singing, pinging noises as creatures moved around on it or dived through it. 'Herons mostly. They'll have a go.'

'OK—that's one predator too many!' Danny was still shaking after the crocodile scare. 'We've got to get somewhere safe!'

'We're probably safer here than anywhere else,' said Josh. 'We can just wait here until the SWITCH wears off and then we'll splash up out of the water when we turn back into boys.'

'Haven't you forgotten something?' asked Danny. 'Eeeyah!' He jumped as two small but very ugly wiggly brown things swam past, both staring at him with big dull eyes and grimacing with sharp spiky teeth.

'Watchoo lookin' at?' one of them said and then vanished under some boggy leafy stuff.

'Innit?' said the other, as it followed.

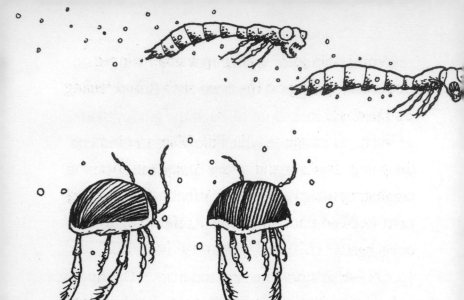

'Dragonfly nymphs,' explained Josh. 'Don't mind them. They've got issues. They're going to be gorgeous one day but for now they've got a face like a smashed toilet.'

'Ri-ight,' said Danny. 'But not predators, eh?'

'Nah—we could have 'em if we wanted. Although they'd put up a fight,' said Josh, happily. It was a wonderful experience to be at the top of the food chain for a change.

'Anyway,' went on Danny, clinging to the rock alongside Josh, 'I said, aren't you forgetting something?'

'What?' said Josh, eyeing up a small winged creature struggling on the pond surface and feeling a bit peckish.

'Well . . . let me see . . . Biff, Ollie, and Milo—the pocket freaks—and *lovely* Poppy with her fascinating tub of ants' eggs? What are *they* going to make of you and me suddenly shooting up out of the water? Eh? We'll get banned from Wild Things—definitely!'

Josh ran his front leg across his mouth parts and managed to crease his beetly face into a worried frown. 'It is going to be hard to explain,' he agreed. 'But they've probably nearly finished the pond dipping now. They'll go back inside, soon, to look at what they've got.'

Danny gazed up through the skin of the pond surface and saw vague shapes and colours moving around. It wasn't unpleasant, sitting here in the pond. OK, the inhabitants weren't too pretty, but at least they weren't trying to snack on him.

'Ooh—ooh! Come and see this!' said Josh, pushing off the rock and scudding towards some green and brown stems which snaked up through the water and connected with big, round, flat green and pink platforms on the surface. Lily pads, Danny worked out. Among the stems were some clumps of fine drifting weed and there was a large silvery bubble lodged in one of these drifts.

'Come on,' called Josh and half of him vanished inside the bubble. Danny hurried after him, noticing another one of those weird nymphs gurning at them from under a stick.

PLOLLOP! With great surprise Danny found himself looking into a little dry chamber, rather like a diving bell, with a green stick running up through it. Josh was gazing around it, only his head and two front legs poking into the bubble. It wasn't big enough for them to get right into it.

'What is it?' breathed Danny. His voice sounded more normal without all the water pressing in on them.

'It's someone's home,' whispered Josh. He noticed some little silky threads wound around the green stick and a small bundle, wrapped tightly in white strands, among them. He wondered whether he should tell Danny what it was. Danny would probably freak out.

'*Whose* home?' asked Danny. But he didn't need to ask. The home-owner was getting back from work. A long, fine brown leg pierced the wall of the air pocket, followed by another. And another.

'Oh . . . I don't like this,' gulped Danny. The elegant shape of the legs—four of them now— and the fine hairs running along them, looked horribly familiar.

All of a sudden, with a 'thwip', four more legs, a brown body and several eyes arrived too. The face around the eyes looked none too pleased to see them there.

'*SPIDER!!!*' shrieked Danny, trying to hide behind Josh. He knew he shouldn't be afraid any more—after all, he had *been* a spider, and he knew they were amazing creatures. It was just hard to forget that he'd once nearly had his insides slurped out like soup from a flask by one of these creatures, while he was a bluebottle trapped in a web.

The spider stared at them and they stared back.

'It's OK,' whispered Josh. 'She can't get us. We can eat *her*!'

The spider reared up with her front legs and said, 'Well, I call that *rude*!'

'Oh,' Josh looked very surprised—his feelers shot up like astonished eyebrows. 'Sorry. I didn't think you could understand us. The last spider we met didn't speak English . . . '

'Well—I can!' huffed the spider, her mouth parts flipping about like twitchy fingers. 'And if you *think* you can eat me, just try it!'

'Nah . . . not really very hungry, thanks,' said Josh and edged backwards out of the air pocket.

Danny continued to stare, appalled, at the spider, as she glared back at him angrily. Then he was dragged suddenly out of her home by his rear end, and delivered back into the water world by his brother. 'SPIDERS!' he yelled at Josh. 'You didn't tell me there were spiders—down *here*!'

'Sorry,' said Josh. 'Water spiders. They're brilliant, though, aren't they? I love that little air pod. Brilliant! This is the best thing we've been!'

Danny shuddered. . . But scooting powerfully through the water *was* pretty cool. He began to relax and enjoy himself. 'Anything else good about us?' he asked.

'We-ell,' said Josh. 'There's something you should probably know. It's happened before and we were fine, so don't freak out.'

'What?' demanded Danny, his antennae twitching nervously.

'We're girls again.'

'NO! No—I refuse to be a girl again!'

'It's no big deal,' said Josh, scooting on through the golden-green underwater glade. 'When you were an ant girl you'd never have known if I hadn't told you.'

'Apart from all the giggling,' grunted Danny.

'Well... yeah, there was the giggling,' grinned Josh.

'How do you know we're girls?' demanded Danny.

'It's our go faster stripes,' explained Josh. 'You don't get 'em on boy great diving beetles. Just the girls. Let it go, Danny.'

Danny shuddered again. And this time the water shuddered around him. Then it shuddered again. A very BIG shudder.

Josh and Danny spun about and stared at each other. 'What's that?' whispered Josh, sounding scared for the first time.

Suddenly there was an ear-splitting crash and the water churned about wildly, sending them spinning away from each other. Dancing fragments of light, waterweed, and tiny see-through creatures flew in all directions and Danny felt himself being thrown around uncontrollably.

He shut his eyes, hoping he was returning to being a boy—and that nobody would see. But when at last the storm around him calmed down, he realized he was still a great diving beetle. Light streamed all around him in a very odd way. It was coming from above—and around—and underneath. He tried to swim through it and find Josh but—CRACK—his head whacked into a solid forcefield which sent him spinning back again. What? Danny tried again. CRACK! And then he understood why it was so bright and why he couldn't travel for even three pushes of his legs before being smacked in the face.

He was in a jar.

He had been pond dipped.

Dippy Chick

Josh lay on his back, waving his legs in the air. For a few seconds he thought he must have morphed back into being a boy. He waited for everyone to start shouting at him for falling in the pond.

But after a few seconds he opened his eyes and realized he was still a beetle. A beetle on its back. On the bank of the pond. A flash of white and grey zoomed across the blue sky. A heron? Josh let off a killer guff and flipped himself over onto his front. He scurried under the shelter of a rocky outcrop, gasping with shock (and disgust— wow—that guff was *awful*!). Now, he thought, as he surveyed the nearby water and the clumps of bog weed, *where* was Danny?

'Oooooh!' came a familiar voice. 'Oooh, Scratch, look! Someone's left chocolate cake! Look! Oh, it's our lucky day!'

Josh peered around the edge of the rock and
saw two brown rats sniffing at something in the
undergrowth, not far from the picnic bench, which
now rose up like a huge wooden monolith. 'WAIT!
STOP!' yelled Josh, scurrying towards the rats.
'DON'T EAT THAT!'

The rats paused and looked over towards him.
'What's *that* about?' murmured one of them.

'Oh, I expect he wants a bit for himself. Well,
tough luck!' said the other one, turning back to the
crumbly brown treat.

'SCRATCH! SNIFF! STOP!' bellowed Josh and all of a sudden he found himself up in the air. His wings had shot out of their cases and he was flying, low to the ground, straight for the rats. He had to save them from being SWITCHed. After all—they'd saved him and Danny from death quite a few times!

'Josh? Is that you?' asked Sniff, her delicate spray of whiskers twitching as she peered at the beetle flying towards her. 'Oh my! What has she changed you into this time?' Scratch and Sniff knew all about Petty and her SWITCH spray.

They had spent time in her lab, listening in as she talked loudly to herself.

'Yes—yes it is me,' said Josh, landing at their feet. 'And you *mustn't* eat that cake! Petty's put SWITCH pellets in it! That's how I ended up like this.'

'Oh, you poor love!' clucked Sniff. 'She just keeps getting you, doesn't she?'

Josh sighed. 'Well, she doesn't *deliberately* try to get us—it just seems to keep happening!'

Sniff gave her husband a *look* and he shrugged back at her. 'Whatever you say, dear,' she said to Josh and then gazed sadly at the cake. Sniff *loved* chocolate cake. Danny or Josh occasionally put some under the shed in their back garden, where Scratch and Sniff lived, and sometimes the rats would come out to eat it with them. When they were in boy form, Danny and Josh couldn't understand what the rats said, but the happy waves of thanks worked well enough.

'Such a shame,' sighed Sniff, turning her back firmly on the contaminated cake. 'But where's your brother?'

'That's just it,' said Josh. He looked around anxiously. 'I don't know. He was in the pond with me and then there was a big sort of waterquake and now he's gone.'

'Well—that's what caused your waterquake,' said Scratch, pointing his brown furry paw at the looming shapes that moved around the pond. 'Your human friends were splashing about in the water with jars.'

Josh gulped. 'Oh. Oh *no*. They were pond dipping! What if Danny's been pond dipped?'

'Well, he might not have been, love,' said Sniff, with a reassuring smile which revealed her long yellow front teeth. 'He might just still be in the water, wondering where you are.'

Josh stared at the large green lake. It was going to take a while to search through it. It was probably a better idea to check the pond-dipping jars first. He could fly into the wildlife centre building and have a quick look, and if Danny wasn't in a jar he could zip back to the pond and look for him there. Of course, Danny might just turn back into a boy at any time and burst out of the pond anyway. And

Josh knew he could change at any time too. He would have to be careful to land as soon as he felt that peculiar feeling which came just before the change back occurred.

Then Josh shivered.

'What's up, mate?' asked Scratch.

'If Danny is in a glass jar . . . ' murmured Josh, ' . . . what's going to happen to him when he changes back to being a boy?'

The rats and the beetle stared at each other, looking as worried as it's possible for two rats and a beetle to look.

'You'd better get going!' advised Scratch. 'We'll stay here for a while, in case you need us.'

'OW!' Danny's head smacked against the lid of the jar. He had remembered that he had wings, shaken them out of their cases, and then tried to fly up out of the captured pond water. But he'd only succeeded in knocking himself silly and sploshing back down again.

He noticed something looking at him. It was one of the ugly little dragonfly nymphs. 'Watchoo tryin'a do?' it sneered at him. 'You is mad, innit?'

Danny ignored it and eyed the lid of the jar through the ever-shifting water. The jar itself had been set down now, on an orange shelf. Danny knew it must have been put into the learning centre. He could just make out the room beyond his curved glass prison. *How* was he going to get out of here?

'No good tryin'a git aht, innit,' said the nymph. 'Weez well prizzed up.'

'No—I can fly out!' argued Danny.

'Me too, bruv,' warbled the nymph. 'Just gotta wait a while. Deze wings'll be full growed in a while, innit.'

Of course, remembered Danny, Josh had said these weird little creepy-crawlies turned into dragonflies. This one didn't look as if he was going to change any time soon though. Danny gulped. *He* could change at any moment, he suddenly realized. Back to a full-sized eight year old. But what if he changed now? While he was trapped in a glass jar? What would that do to him? What would give? The glass? Or *him*?

Danny stared out into the wavy lines of the room where he'd hung around, bored, only minutes ago. He thought he had, truly, never been more terrified. There was a musical thud on the other side of the glass as the string attached to the jar flopped down across it. It was pink string.

Danny gulped again. He had seen that pink string before. Where . . . ?

You don't want to know! whispered a voice in his head.

Then a giant, warped, freckly face suddenly wrapped itself around the jar, grinning and steaming up the glass.

No no no, whimpered the voice in Danny's

head. *I said you didn't want to know!*

But Danny *did* know. It was too late to block out the awful truth. Poppy had caught him in her pond-dipping jar. Poppy might very well be taking Danny home . . .

Important Points

Petty Potts sat in the sun and watched a pair of rats under the picnic bench, through her binoculars. They were definitely sniffing around the SWITCH pellet infested cake.

'Come on! Why aren't you eating it?' she whispered, tapping on the little plastic tub she had brought to collect newly morphed creatures in. She usually had a few seconds to get them while they flapped about in confusion.

Petty huffed to herself. Nothing was going to plan today. She really hadn't *meant* for Josh and Danny to end up getting SWITCHed again. It was all Danny's fault for being such a greedy little so and so. She hoped the brothers were getting along OK as great diving beetles. At least they were a bit less likely to get eaten this time—there wasn't much in a pond which would take on such a ferocious predator.

It was a relief when all the children finished their pond dipping and went back inside. At least when Josh and Danny morphed back into human form again they wouldn't be in full view of all their friends and the grown-ups who ran the Wild Things group. Petty knew she must sit tight and wait for Josh and Danny to come back. They would need help in explaining what had happened to them and Petty would have to come up with something to convince everyone that they had just fallen into the pond . . . probably while helping her to retrieve her hat or something. Petty took off her hat and threw it out onto the pond, just in case.

She looked at the rats again, while she waited. They were still not eating the cake. Rats, though, were very intelligent. Maybe they'd smelt something and decided not to take the risk. Not that being very intelligent always helped you through life, reflected Petty, with a sigh. *She* was super-intelligent, but had still got tricked by her old friend, Victor Crouch, when they worked together in the government's top secret underground labs.

If Victor hadn't stolen her work and burnt out her memory so he could not be caught, she wouldn't be sitting here now, worrying about Josh and Danny. She would have carried on with developing the REPTOSWITCH spray, as well as the BUGSWITCH spray. She would be the most famous scientist in the world.

'Still—*Victor* isn't the most famous scientist in the world either, is he?' muttered Petty to herself, with a smile. 'No, Victor! You messed up! What you didn't know was that I always suspected someone would try to steal my work, and so I faked all my paper codes and put the *real* codes into my cubes. My wonderful cubes!'

But Petty frowned now. Because although she had all the BUGSWITCH cubes and could make her sprays using the code hidden inside them, the REPTOSWITCH code was not yet complete. She had only five cubes, each with a beautiful hologram of a reptile twinkling in its glass centre. Josh and Danny had not yet found the sixth. With parts of her memory burnt out, Petty just didn't

remember where she'd hidden the cubes. Josh and
Danny had managed to find most of them . . . but
without the last, she would never be able to make
any REPTOSWITCH spray.

'Oooooh!' Petty slapped her forehead. 'Why did
you have to get your memory burnt out, you fool?'
she hissed at herself.

A man standing in the bush behind her
scratched his chin with a pointed black fingernail
and grinned to himself, before moving silently back
to the pond dippers in the learning room.

Josh flew into the Wildlife Centre learning room, aghast at the amount of noise his wings were making. They were whirring and buzzing, the way beetles' wings often do. He just had to hope that it wasn't very loud to human ears. The last thing he needed was for some fascinated Wild Thing to spot him and try to catch him.

He could see his fellow Wild Things dotted around the room—huge lumps of colourful human, ambling about and making a lot of noise. Good! The noise would hopefully disguise the sound his wings were making. The pond dippers had all come back into the learning room now, and put their jars in a row along an orange shelf, ready to be inspected. Poppy's grandfather was already peering into them, holding a notebook and pencil and tapping against the jars with one peculiar pointed black fingernail. Josh flew high over his head, wishing the old man would move away so he could inspect the jars for signs of Danny.

Then Poppy ran up to her grandfather and grabbed hold of his hand. The old man turned away and Josh flew down to the jars and began to work his way along them all. Most of them had lots of weed, a couple of water snails, and not much else. Most of the pond creatures were way too quick to get caught out by pond dippers. The third jar along, with the pink string on it, had a bone-crunchingly ugly face peering out of it, through a drift of green weed. A dragonfly nymph. It saw Josh peering in at it and mouthed 'Watchoo lookin' at?' Josh was just about to move on when another face suddenly bloomed through the weed. A great diving beetle.

'Josh! Is that you?!' mouthed the beetle and Josh could just about hear Danny's voice behind the glass.

'Yes! It's me!' he called back. 'Danny! You've got to get out of there!'

'*Tell* me about it!' yelled Danny. 'It's no fun being stuck in here with nymphy boy!'

'Is youz dissin' me?' demanded Nymphy Boy.

'I can't get out!' yelled Danny. 'I've tried to fly up but the lid's on!'

Josh landed on the lid. It had a couple of air holes punched through the tin, but they were too small to get through—and there was no way he could twist off the lid.

'Come on, Josh! Think of something!' begged Danny. 'A few more minutes and there's going to be some very nasty jam in this jar!'

'I'll have to get help!' cried Josh, through the air holes. 'Scratch and Sniff are out by the pond—and Petty—somehow I'll have to get them to help. Just . . . don't go anywhere . . .'

'Oh, all right. As you've asked so nicely—I'll just stay here then!' snapped Danny.

Nymphy Boy loomed up at him, looking even uglier, and spat: 'I iz not a boy. I iz a *girl*.'

'Yeah,' muttered Danny, with a wince. 'Me too, sister.'

Jarring Moments

'Scratch! Sniff! I've found Danny!' gasped Josh as he landed under the picnic table in a spray of dust and grass seeds.

'Good!' said Sniff.

'*Not* good!' said Josh. 'He's in a jam! Worse . . . he's in a jam *jar*. He's stuck inside it with the lid on. I can't get it off. And he could change back into being a boy at any moment and then . . . and then . . .'

'*Squelch,*' shuddered Scratch. Sniff elbowed him in his furry chest and glared at him.

'How can we get it open?' asked Josh.

'Well,' said Scratch. 'I don't know if we can open it, but we can certainly knock it off the shelf and smash it. Would that help?'

Josh stared at them. 'It's not the *best* way out,'

he said. 'But it's better than nothing.' He just
hoped that Danny wouldn't get cut in half by
shattered glass.

'No time to lose then,' said Scratch, and he and
Sniff ran towards the learning room.

'Be careful!' Josh yelled after them. He knew
what they were doing was very dangerous for
them. The Wildlife Centre staff could try to trap
them if they saw them. Rats might be wildlife too,
but the people at the Centre said there were too
many and numbers had to be kept down. Rising
up in the air, Josh scouted around for the root of all
these disasters—Petty Potts. He saw her sitting on
a bench by the pond. Without her usual hat, her
silvery hair was blowing around her head.

He buzzed down in front of her face. She didn't flap him away but sat up straight. 'Danny? Josh? Is that you?' she said, in a voice which came out loud, deep, and boomy to Josh's beetle ears.

'Follow me!' shouted Josh, although he knew Petty would only hear a buzzing noise. Her giant human ears weren't set up to hear such tiny creatures. If only he could just switch back to human now and explain, life would be much easier—but it was never possible to predict exactly when the change back would happen. And he didn't know how much SWITCH pellet he had eaten compared to Danny. It could be either one of them first . . .

He turned and flew back to the learning room after Scratch and Sniff. It looked as if the rats were Danny's only chance.

'Where'th Danny gone?' said Poppy to the other Wild Things. 'And where'th Josh?'

'I reckon they both went off round the back,' said Milo, busy writing notes on his worksheet.

'Well, they thould be back now!' said Poppy, looking annoyed. 'I wanted to thow Danny my pond life, Grandad!' she said to the man in the hat. He took his hat off and rubbed around where his eyebrows should have been, and then put the hat back on again.

'Yes, Poppy,' he smiled. 'And I really wanted to meet Danny, too. And Josh. Don't they live over in Chestnut Lane?'

'Yeth,' said Poppy. She led Grandfather over to the rows of jars and then let out a little shriek. Two furry shapes had just shot up the wall and onto the shelf.

'UGH!' shrieked one of the ladies handing out worksheets. 'RATS!'

There were more screams and then a crash as the rats bashed one of the jars off the shelf and onto the floor, spilling pond water, weed, and three water snails across the tiles. Then another jar toppled over. This one had pink string on it.

'Oh help! That'th my jar!' squeaked Poppy.

'Oh help!' gurgled Danny as he tumbled through a twisting vortex of water, weed, and madness. The jar was falling. He was a second away from being in a broken glass and pondweed stew. Maybe he'd make it though . . . maybe he'd be able to fly away.

WHOMP! SLOOSH!

Suddenly the jam jar stopped falling. A storm of water churned up, down, and around and then Danny realized the glass was still intact. A hand grasped it firmly, pale long fingers wrapping around. One black, pointy fingernail tapped against the glass.

'Thankyou, Grandad!' squeaked Poppy.

Just outside the window, Josh saw the old man in the hat stop Danny's jar from falling. 'Oh no!' he moaned, hovering up and down with his wings in a frenzy. 'How will we get Danny out now?'

Then he crashed onto the decking below with a loud thud. Everyone in the learning room ran to the window and the door to see what had just fallen. An eight-year-old boy lay on his back, his arms and legs flapping, looking dazed and confused.

'Josh?' said Poppy.

'You all right?' said Milo.

Josh saw Poppy's grandfather lean out behind her, the jam jar still swinging in his hand. He knew it was now or never, while he still had them all surprised and confused. He leaped to his feet, snatched the jam jar from the old man, and ran across the wildflower meadow before anyone could stop him.

Victor-y

For Danny, it was like being in the spin cycle of a washing machine. He no longer knew which way was up. Every so often he would collide with the nymph, who was too dazed herself to say anything. There wasn't time to breathe, let alone menace anyone.

'OI! COME BACK HERE!' yelled the old man, who was chasing after Josh. 'Come back here with that jar!'

Blimey, thought Josh. He knew it was Poppy's jar, and the old man was her grandad, but he couldn't believe there was a chase going on over a bit of pond weed! Only he knew how special the stuff in the jar was. He needed to get it open now—before Danny changed back. He had to stop running, even if Poppy's grandad caught up.

Josh ducked behind a tree and undid the lid. He tipped the frothy green mess out onto the grass and Danny slid out, landing on his back. His legs were not wiggling. He was quite still.

'DANNY! DANNY!' yelled Josh. He wanted to pick the beetle up and shake it—make it come alive. But he might just squash it in all his upset. 'DANNY!' sobbed Josh. 'DANNY—PLEASE DON'T BE DEAD!'

'Let me see,' said a voice. And Petty Potts knelt down beside him. She put her face close to the soggy beetle and then blew on it. The legs waved. But that might just have been in the breeze. Petty looked up at Josh, who was holding his hands over his mouth and blinking with shock. She blew on Danny again. This time a feeler twitched. Then a leg.

Then Danny thumped Petty in the face.

'Ow!' said Petty, holding her nose. 'That's the second time you've lumped me on the nose this month!' But she was grinning with relief. Getting whacked in the face as Danny bounced back to boy shape was a price she was willing to pay.

Danny sat up, his clothes soggy and covered with pondweed. He looked at the jar, which lay at an angle with just a little weed left in it. 'Oh,' he said. 'What happened to Nymphy Girl?'

'You what?' gasped Josh.

'There was one of those dragonfly nymphs in there with me. Is she all right?' Danny peered into the sludgy weed. He could just make out a tiny, angry face. He chuckled. 'We have to put her back,' he said.

'Are you telling me that you care about a dragonfly nymph?' said Josh.

'Well—you don't have to make a big thing of it,' said Danny, emptying the jar into a nearby watery ditch. 'She wasn't my girlfriend. Not really my type. No need to get excited.'

'Oh, I don't know,' came a strange voice. 'I think there's a lot to get excited about.'

Everyone stared up into the pale face of the man in the hat. He was smiling down at the scene around the spilt pond water and scratching the area where his eyebrows should have been with one black, pointed fingernail.

Petty gasped and stood up. 'YOU!' she said 'YOU! VICTOR CROUCH!'

Josh and Danny gaped at each other. They had never really believed that Victor Crouch existed.

They had thought he was all part of Petty's mad imagination. But here he stood, large as life.

'Hello, Petty,' smiled Victor. 'You remember me, then.'

'Remember you? Why, of course I do, you snake!' she spat. 'Victor Crouch—my old friend—the one who tried to steal my work and burn out my memory!'

Victor sighed. 'Aaaah, Petty! Still so lovely when you're angry. But you've got it all wrong. Somebody did burn out your memory, that's true. And that's why you can't remember who. It wasn't me. I am your friend.'

Petty narrowed her eyes at him.

'Your *friend*,' repeated Victor. 'And I've come to take you back with me! The government wants you back. We all missed you and your genius brain so much. It's all been a big mistake.'

Petty tilted her head to one side, thinking about Victor Crouch's words. She rummaged around in her pockets absent-mindedly.

'We're still trying to find out who *did* burn out your memory,' said Victor. 'And what he did

with your work . . . the cubes . . . Petty? The
BUGSWITCH cubes and the REPTOSWITCH
cubes? Remember? You told me all about them.
Where did you find them in the end? Obviously
you've got the spray working . . . ' He waved his
pointy fingernail at Danny and Josh. 'Your little
friends have been having creepy-crawly adventures
with you, haven't they? What brilliant work!'

Petty stared at him. Then she smiled. 'Oh,
Victor! How could I have been so wrong about
you?'

Josh and Danny pulled faces at each other.

Surely Petty wasn't falling for this? Victor Crouch was so creepy he made a slug look good.

'You're not the man I thought you were,' sighed Petty. 'You're not that at all! You're a COCKROACH! THAT'S WHAT YOU ARE!'

Victor's charming smile vanished. 'All right— have it your way, you mad old witch!' and he pulled a hand-held radio communicator out of his pocket. 'I have agents everywhere! All I have to do is call them and you'll be locked away for ever!' He went to press the button on the radio.

There was a short sharp hiss. Petty stood with a spray bottle in her hands and Victor froze as a pale yellow mist of SWITCH landed on him.

'What? What have you done?' he gasped.

'I told you,' said Petty. 'You're a cockroach.'

Victor vanished. There was a shimmy of shiny black wing case in the grass. Petty lifted her foot above it.

'Well,' she said. 'Nice to catch up on old times, Victor. Cheerio!'

But before her foot could stamp down, Danny leapt forward and pushed her sideways. 'PETTY! NO!'

'He's EVIL!' insisted Petty, peering in alarm at the grass. 'He'll have us all kidnapped and tortured for the SWITCH secrets! He cannot be allowed to escape!'

'But that would be murder!' said Danny. 'You can't kill people! Not deliberately!'

'Probably wouldn't have worked anyway,' said Josh. 'Have you ever tried to kill a cockroach? They're armour plated. They'd survive a nuclear fall out. They can live for three months without their *heads*. And you'll *never* splat them on a soft surface.'

Petty dropped to her knees and rummaged in the grass. 'He's gone! He's gone already! How could you let him escape? How could you?'

Whose Grandad?

'Well . . . at least he's not going to bother us for a
while,' said Josh, staring into the grass. 'And maybe
he'll get eaten anyway . . .'

'I certainly hope so,' grumbled Petty, putting the
spray bottle back in her pocket. 'Good job I had
some spare spray with me. You never know when
you might need it.' She picked up the walky-talky
radio which Victor Crouch must have dropped as
he turned into a cockroach. 'Don't look at me like
that! You heard what he said. If he'd pressed the
button on this radio and called all his agents, we'd
be on our way to a deep, dark prison by now.'

'What? Us?' said Danny. 'But we're just kids.
Nobody would lock us up!'

'Don't you believe it,' said Petty. 'They would
know that you know what I know, don't you

know? And if you know, they would want to know what you know and there's no knowing what they'd do to know you know!'

Danny and Josh edged away from her.

'You're barmy,' said Danny. 'We don't want to play with you any more! No more helping you out. No more hunting for REPTOSWITCH cubes. You're nuts and you've just tried to kill a man.'

'A cockroach,' said Petty. 'I tried to kill a cockroach. I'm sorry you're upset. Come and see me tomorrow and we'll all have some cake and feel much better.'

'I've gone off your cake,' said Danny.

'Me too,' said Josh.

They turned and ran.

'I always knew this would end in trouble!' puffed Josh as they arrived back at the Wildlife Centre. 'And what are we going to say to Poppy? How will we explain what happened to her grandad?'

Poppy was happily doing a drawing of a dragonfly when they got back to the learning room. 'Oh, there you are!' she beamed as they came in.

'What happened to you? Did you fall in the pond and get thoaked?'

'Yes,' said Josh.

'Er . . . Poppy,' said Danny. 'About your grandad . . . um . . . did you see where he went?'

Poppy looked up from her drawing. 'My grandad? He'th at home with my gran, thilly!'

'But—but he was just here,' said Danny, confused. 'He caught your jam jar, remember!'

'Oh, that wasn't my grandad!' said Poppy.

'What?' gasped Josh and Danny, together.

'I never met him until today,' she said, going back to her drawing. 'He just said he was helping out and that everyone called him "Grandad". Why? Is he *your* grandad?'

'No—no, never saw him before . . . ' murmured Danny. He and Josh sank down on to the chairs next to Poppy, feeling tired and confused.

'Do you like my drawing?' she said to Danny, holding up the paper proudly. It was a good drawing.

'Yeah—it's great,' he said.

'I *like* you!' beamed Poppy. 'You're thutch fun!

Here—you can have thith!' And she dug her hand in her pocket and pulled out a little plastic bag. 'I found thith in your road yethterday. You can have it!'

Danny undid the plastic bag and stared in wonder at the thing in his hand.

'Thankth . . . I mean, thanks, Poppy,' he said and wandered out of the Wildlife Centre with Josh at his side trying to look into his palm.

Danny gazed around.
There was no sign of Petty,
or—of course—Victor. He
opened his hand and showed
Josh. It was a cube. A shiny, glass cube,
with a hologram of a chameleon twinkling inside it.

The very last cube, containing the last vital part
of the code for Petty's REPTOSWITCH spray.

Josh and Danny looked at each other. After all
their adventures as creepy-crawlies, after all the
times they'd nearly been squashed or eaten, after
all the amazing things they'd done, like fly and leap
and walk upside down and swim under water . . .
NOW, they could move on to being something
else even more amazing.

REPTILES.

'But we've just seen Petty try to squash a man
dead under her heel,' said Josh. 'I don't think we
should give her this. I don't think we should have
anything more to do with her.'

'Yes,' said Danny. 'I think you're right.' He shoved
the cube deep into his pocket. 'Come on, Mum
should be waiting for us in the car park now.'

'Yeah,' said Josh, trying to sound normal. 'Yeah, we can see her new car! We can have a ride in it and forget everything that's just happened. And pretend it never did happen. That's the best thing!'

They walked round to the car park at the front of the Blackthorn Wildlife Centre and there was Mum, tooting her horn and waving from her new, shiny green car.

'Look! Look, boys!' she grinned. 'Come and get in! I've got a Beetle!'

DIARY ENTRY *621.4

SUBJECT: VICTOR CROUCH IS (POSSIBLY) DEAD!

I cannot believe it! I very nearly KILLED Victor Crouch! I had that nasty little cockroach right under my heel—and then that blasted Danny stopped me! He and Josh seemed to think I was the maniac.

I tried to explain that Victor would have had us all banged up in a government prison for the rest of our lives if he had caught us and told his agents what we knew. But now he's escaped and if he doesn't get eaten he will certainly be back.

S.W.I.T.C.H

$$\frac{4 \times \pi^2}{0S-7*} \quad \sqrt{\frac{P_2}{0.8}} \times \frac{V_6^2 0/9}{9\sqrt{50}} = \frac{4.198}{4.197} \frac{}{(548)}$$

I do hope Josh and Danny will come round tomorrow so I can explain again. They have to understand the DANGER we're all in!

And of course, I really need their help. We still haven't found the last REPTOSWITCH cube and without it I can go no further. I'm sure I will manage to talk them round. After all, they both can't wait to try out being a giant python or an alligator or a monitor lizard.

All boys want that. And even boys who worry about silly things like me stamping on a cockroach will want to be a reptile too much to worry for long. Won't they ...?

Chin up, Petty. They'll be back.

$\dfrac{60}{\text{OUP}} \to \not\!\!\text{x} \to \tfrac{1}{2}st$

REMEMBER

PLACES TO VISIT

Want to brush up on your bug knowledge?
Here's a list of places with special areas dedicated
to creepy-crawlies.

Liverpool Museum

http://www.liverpoolmuseums.org.uk/wml/
naturalworld/bughouse/

Marwell Wildlife Park

http://www.marwell.org.uk/

Natural History Museum

http://www.nhm.ac.uk/

Remember, you don't need
to go far to find your favourite
bugs. Why not venture out
into your garden or the
park and see how many
different creatures
you can spot.

WEBSITES

Find out more about nature and wildlife
using the websites below.

http://www.bbc.co.uk/cbbc/wild/

http://www.nhm.ac.uk/kids-only/

http://kids.nationalgeographic.com/

http://www.switch-books.co.uk/

Find out how the S.W.I.T.C.H.
adventures began . . .

Ali Sparkes

Winner of the Blue Peter Book of the Year

Illustrated by
Ross Collins

S.W.I.T.C.H.

SERUM WHICH INSTIGATES TOTAL CELLULAR HIJACK

Spider Stampede

Losing Piddle

'AAAAAAARRRRRGGGGHHHHHH!!!!'

'GETITOFF—GETITOFF—

GETITOFFMEEEE!!!!'

Josh looked up from his book to see his twin brother running round in circles by the hedge, wearing nothing but swimming trunks and a look of panic.

Oh no—not true.

He was also wearing a spider.

'DON'T just sit there!' squeaked Danny, as he whirled about. 'Get it OFF!'

Josh sighed and put his book down on the grass. It was amazing, he thought, that the spider could possibly hang on while his brother was thrashing about so wildly. It was a garden spider and quite large—probably female. It had run up Danny's arm when he went to pick up his water pistol and then scarpered over his shoulder. Josh knew this because of the kind of dance his brother had just done across the grass. A sort of backwards shimmy, with gasps of horror, followed by madly flapping arms and then the whirling as his unwelcome passenger legged it down his shoulder blade.

'You should go in for the Under Nines Disco Championship,' Josh said, as he dodged under a flailing arm to scoop up the dizzy spider, now hanging on to the waistband of Danny's trunks.

'Oh very funny!' squealed Danny. 'Have you got it? Is it gone?!'

'Yes—calm down. Look! She's a beauty!' Josh cupped the spider in his hands and held it out for Danny to see. It was nut brown with mottled yellow patterns on its back.

'NOOO! Get it away from me!'

'But look—she's got these amazing feet that can hook on to stuff while she's hanging upside down and—'

'Just STOP talking about the S-P-I-D-E-R!'

growled Danny. He shuddered and refused to look while Josh gently dropped it behind the shed.

'She'll be back over by the hedge again in no time,' said Josh, which didn't comfort his twin much. 'Along with all the others. You're never more than a few feet away from a spider, you know.'

'Not *one* more *word* to do with . . . those . . . *things*!'

Josh pushed his hands into his shorts pockets

and grinned. 'Mandibles,' he muttered, quietly. He didn't think Danny would know what this word was. He'd read only yesterday that 'mandibles' were what spiders used for eating. Not teeth exactly— just sort of munchy bits on their faces.

Danny hated anything creepy-crawly. For twins, he and Josh were very different. Josh was fascinated by small creatures and bugs. He had loads of wildlife books. He used to bring woodlice, snails, and beetles into the house, but after Jenny, their older sister, found earwigs in her hairdryer and then Danny screamed loud enough to wake the dead after stepping into his brother's box of centipedes when he got up for the toilet in the middle of the night, Mum said Josh could only look at bugs and stuff outside. It was probably just as well because if Jenny didn't squash them flat with a sandal, Mum would suck them up in the vacuum cleaner—or Piddle would eat them. Piddle, their scruffy little terrier (named after a habit he had when he got overexcited) liked nothing more than to munch up a spider if he spotted one sauntering by.

'How can you *like* those things?' Danny asked,

pulling his shorts and T-shirt on over his swimming trunks. He'd gone off the paddling pool—too many dead flies in it. 'Eeeuuw! I wish there weren't any insects in the world!'

'One—spiders aren't insects, they're arachnids,' said Josh, getting up onto the climbing frame, 'and two, if there were no insects in the world we would all die out. The human race depends on them.'

'You freaky little bug boffin!' muttered Danny.

'Lucky for you that I *do* like them!' added Josh. 'Or we'd *both* be screaming and disco-dancing all over the garden right now.'

Danny ignored him—but he checked his spiky fair hair with a shiver, just in case another spider had dropped in. Josh's hair was short and neat and he wouldn't mind a spider in it at all. How could twins be so un-alike? wondered Danny as he pulled on his trainers. He loved playing computer games and listening to loud music. Josh would rather play with newts and listen to birdsong.

But, Danny had to admit, he *was* useful for creepy-crawly removal.

Danny abandoned the water pistol and picked

up his skateboard. Soon he was pelting up and
down the path with Piddle racing along beside
him, yapping and nearly tripping him up every ten
seconds.

Upstairs, from Jenny's bedroom window, a
pop tune thumped loudly, while from the kitchen
poured the burble of daytime TV, which their mum
liked to watch while she did the ironing.

From the other side of the high wooden fence
there came a thump. And then another thump.
And then a crotchety voice. '*Will* you all shut up!
I'd have a quieter afternoon on the main runway
at Heathrow Airport!' Josh grimaced. It was Miss

Potts who lived in the run-down red-brick house next door. People thought she was a bit eccentric. An old misery more like, thought Josh.

'I SAID,' came the voice again, louder. 'Will you all SHUT UP?!'

But Mum and Jenny and Danny and Piddle were all making way too much noise to hear. 'Sorry, Miss Potts,' said Josh, feeling embarrassed. 'I'll ask them to be quieter.'

'Oh, don't bother!' she snapped back, the top of her tweedy hat the only thing he could see over the fence. 'I'll soon be deaf and then it won't matter!'

Josh made flappy 'shushing' movements at Danny and mouthed, 'Miss Potts!'

Danny skidded his skateboard to a halt, shaking his head, and Piddle sat back on his furry bottom and waited, wiggling impatiently, for the fun to start again.

Josh ran past him and pushed the kitchen window shut and at once the noise from Mum's TV programme dropped. He could still hear Miss Potts though, just on the other side of the fence.

She was muttering, 'Remember! Remember! *Oh, you stupid old biddy!* Remember! Where did you hide them? Where?'

Josh bent down and peered through a knothole in the wood and saw the old lady crawling along through the weeds, which were nearly as tall as he was, obviously searching for something. Then she suddenly bobbed up, thwacked her hand hard against her forehead and snapped: 'STUPID old woman! Had to go and get your brain burnt out, didn't you?' Then she stood up and stomped off into her ramshackle garden shed.

It was right what they said about Petty Potts, Josh decided. She really was mad.

'She's always moaning about noise,' Danny said, suddenly, in his ear. Josh jumped. 'Does she think this is a library or something? It's a blummin' garden! Kids play in gardens. Dogs play in gardens!' And he picked up a rubber ball and threw it for Piddle. 'There you go, Piddle! Catch!'

Piddle hurtled down the path and then threw himself into the heap of cuttings and compost in the far corner. 'Don't pay any attention to her—old whinge-pants,' said Danny. 'Come on, Piddle! Here, boy!'

They glanced back down the garden, expecting to see Piddle foraging through the leaves and cut grass—and then they both blinked, and stared back at each other in surprise.

Piddle had vanished.

FUN AND GAMES

There are more games for you to play and download free on the S.W.I.T.C.H. website.
www.switch-books.co.uk

Word search

Search for the hidden words listed below:

BEETLE	SPIDER
VICTOR	DRAGONFLY
PETTY	JOSH
POPPY	DANNY
NEWT	WILD THINGS

W	S	O	T	Q	H	J	O	S	H
V	I	C	T	O	R	P	A	N	N
T	P	L	C	B	E	E	T	L	E
H	O	E	D	Y	N	T	I	V	E
J	P	R	M	T	P	T	O	I	R
D	P	A	P	P	H	Y	W	L	E
A	Y	S	O	N	Y	I	M	U	D
N	V	P	H	T	W	E	N	F	I
N	I	O	J	S	M	U	L	G	P
Y	L	F	N	O	G	A	R	D	S

Answers on page 120

Spot the difference

These pictures *look* the same, but can you spot ten differences?

Answers on page 120

True or false?

1) Great diving beetles have six legs

2) The great diving beetle has a sting to kill predators

3) Some types of spiders can live under water

4) Great diving beetles have wings

5) Dragonfly nymphs are fully grown

6) Great diving beetles eat small fish

7) Great diving beetles have claws on their front legs
to catch prey

8) If the great diving beetle stopped swimming
it would float to the surface

9) Dragonfly nymphs can fly

10) The great diving beetle uses its front legs to
propel itself through the water

Answers on page 120

Missing pieces

Can you work out which piece of the puzzle is missing?

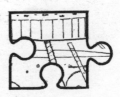

Answer on page 120

Which S.W.I.T.C.H. character are you?

You have a sweet tooth
— no
— yes

You are sporty
— yes
— no

You enjoy plotting and scheming
— no
— yes

You are interested in nature
— no
— yes

You prefer listening to music than reading
— no
— yes

You are untrustworthy
— yes
— yes
— no

You love looking at nature in its natural habitat
— yes

DANNY
You are fun-loving and mischievous. You like adventure and living in the fast lane.

JOSH
You have an inquisitive mind and friends can always rely on you to lend a helping hand if they are in trouble.

VICTOR CROUCH
You are very clever but also very sneaky. You would rather take the credit for another person's hard work than do the work yourself.

Maze

Help Josh and Danny save the dragonfly
nymph from the jar.

Answer on page 121

Board game

You have been turned into a great diving beetle and must search for the missing REPTOSWITCH cube.

For this game you will need one die, a tiddlywink (or something of a similar size) for each player, and two or more players.

START The Pond 1	You shoot through the water. Move ahead 2 squares. 2	 3
  6	 5	 4
You scare off a predator but scoot back 2 squares. 7	 8	You whizz past some moody dragonfly nymphs. Go forward one square. 9
  12	You meet an underwater spider. Miss your next go. 11	 10
You've been pond dipped! Miss your next go 13	 14	**FINISH** Congratulations! You found the next REPTOSWITCH cube! 15

Are you a bug boffin?

Question 1)
JOSH IS A MEMBER OF A NATURE GROUP.
WHAT ARE THEY CALLED?
A) The Freaky Bug Boffins
B) Wild Things
C) Stink Bugs

Question 2)
ONCE JOSH AND DANNY HAVE BEEN
TURNED INTO GREAT DIVING BEETLES,
HOW DO THEY GET SEPARATED?
A) Danny gets pond dipped by Poppy
B) Josh flies off to say hello to Scratch
and Sniff
C) Danny swims away to hide when he
meets an underwater spider

Question 3)
WHY DO JOSH AND DANNY TURN INTO
GREAT DIVING BEETLES?
A) They drink some SWITCH formula
that Petty Potts left lying around
B) They eat a chocolate muffin with a
SWITCH pellet hidden inside
C) Turning into great diving beetles
sounds fun so they ask Petty Potts to
squirt them with SWITCH spray

Question 4)
HOW DO GREAT DIVING BEETLES BREATHE
UNDER WATER?
A) They have little pockets of oxygen on
their bodies
B) They have gills
C) They use a water reed as a snorkel

Question 5)
WHAT IS JOSH AND DANNY'S SECRET
WEAPON WHEN THEY ARE UNDER WATER?
A) They have spikes on their back legs
B) They can burp any predator out of
the water
C) They can let off the most almighty
stink

Question 6)
WHICH CREATURE DOES DANNY GET
STUCK IN A GLASS JAR WITH?
A) Spider
B) Dragonfly nymph
C) Newt

Question 7)
WHAT IS PARTICULARLY UNUSUAL
ABOUT VICTOR CROUCH'S FACE?
A) He has no eyebrows
B) He has several chins
C) He has a huge wart on the end
of his nose

Question 8)
WHAT DOES PETTY DO TO VICTOR
CROUCH AT THE END OF THE STORY?
A) She trips him up and he falls
in the pond
B) She gives him some chocolate
cake with a SWITCH pellet in it and
he turns into a newt
C) She sprays him with her
SWITCH spray and he turns
into a cockroach

Answers on page 121

Answers

Word search (page 112)

W	S	O	T	Q	H	J	O	S	H
V	I	C	T	O	R	P	A	N	N
T	P	L	C	B	E	E	T	L	E
H	O	E	D	Y	N	T	I	V	E
J	P	R	M	T	P	T	O	I	R
D	P	A	P	P	H	Y	W	L	E
A	Y	S	O	N	Y	I	M	U	D
N	V	P	H	T	W	E	N	F	I
N	I	O	J	S	M	U	L	G	P
Y	L	F	N	O	G	A	R	D	S

Spot the difference (page 113)

True or False (page 114)

1) True
2) False
3) True
4) True
5) False
6) True
7) True
8) True
9) False
10) False

Missing pieces (page 115)

h

120

Answers

Maze (page 117)

Are you a bug boffin?
(page 119)

Answer 1) B

Answer 2) A

Answer 3) B

Answer 4) A

Answer 5) C

Answer 6) B

Answer 7) A

Answer 8) C

Give yourself a point for every question you got right.

6–8 POINTS — You are a real bug boffin! Nothing gets past you.

3–5 POINTS — You are SWITCHed on! You enjoy a good adventure.

0–2 POINTS — Oh dear, looks as if you need to brush up on your bug skills! Better luck next time!

About the author

Ali Sparkes grew up in the woods of Hampshire.
Actually, strictly speaking she grew up in a house
in Hampshire. The woods were great but lacked
basic facilities like sofas and a well stocked fridge.
Nevertheless, the woods were where she and
her friends spent much of their time and so Ali
grew up with a deep and abiding love of wildlife.
If you ever see Ali with a large garden spider on
her shoulder she will most likely be screeching
'AAAAAAAAAARRRRRGHGETITOFFME!'

Ali lives in Southampton with her husband and sons
and would never kill a creepy-crawly of any kind. They
are more scared of her than she is of them. (Creepy-
crawlies, not her husband and sons.)

Other books

in the  series

SERUM WHICH INSTIGATES TOTAL CELLULAR HIJACK

Whether you're interested in insects
or terrified of tarantulas, you'll love the
S.W.I.T.C.H. website!

Find out more about the bugs in Josh
and Danny's adventures, enter fantastic
competitions, read the first chapters
of all of the S.W.I.T.C.H. books, and enjoy
creepy-crawly games and activities.

www.switch-books.co.uk